THE ANIMALS SPEAK

A Christmas Eve Legend

by
Marion Dane Bauer

illustrated by
Brittany Baugus

beaming
books
MINNEAPOLIS

Long and long the story has been told . . .

of a young woman,

her husband,

a donkey,

the faithful donkey,

carrying them to their ancestral land.

Long and long the story has been . . .

of shepherds,

angels,

sheep,

the wooly sheep,

grazing in the fields.

Long and long the story . . .

of a star,

magi,

camels,

the swaying camels,

bearing gold and

frankincense and myrrh.

Angels carried the news
to shepherds, and they came.
A star beckoned the magi,
and they came.

No one called the animals,
but they came too.

Long and long . . .

stable,

manger,

and the cows,

the gentle cows.

All stood in silent awe

until the animals found words to praise.

The donkey, the faithful donkey,

the sheep, the wooly sheep,

the camels, the swaying camels,

and the gentle cows.

HE IS HERE! WELCOME!

Long and long and long . . .
the Child.

Now and now, the story is told . . .

of a young woman,

her husband,

a donkey.

Of shepherds,

angels,

sheep.

Now and now, the story . . .

    of a star,

    magi,

    camels,

    of a stable,

    manger,

    cows.

Now we gather
to celebrate the Child.

Our story told,
we go to our beds

to await the stroke

of midnight,

the velvet stroke of midnight

when, once more . . .

. . . the animals speak.

Donkeys waking in stables.

Sheep grazing in pastures.

Camels plodding across deserts.

Cows resting in barns.

Elephants gathered on savannas.

Bears stirring in dens.

Penguins cozied in snow.

Whales swimming in the sea.

All lift their heads
to the starry sky
and cry,

Forever and forever, the story shall be . . .

sung in treetops,

whispered in woods,

bayed in yards,

purred on pillows . . .

and repeated in
home after home after home
by every one of God's creatures.

"The Child is here!
Rejoice!"

For Ron, remembering all our Christmases. —M.D.B.

To Mom and Dad, for your endless love and support. —B.B.

Text copyright © 2021 Marion Dane Bauer
Illustrations copyright © 2021 Beaming Books

Published in 2021 by Beaming Books, an imprint of 1517 Media. All rights reserved.
No part of this book may be reproduced without permission from the publisher.
Email copyright@1517.media. Printed in Canada.

27 26 25 24 23 22 21   1 2 3 4 5 6 7 8

Hardcover ISBN: 978-1-5064-6643-9
Ebook IBSN: 978-1-5064-6688-0

Library of Congress Cataloging-in-Publication Data

Names: Bauer, Marion Dane, author. | Baugus, Brittany, illustrator.
Title: The animals speak / by Marion Dane Bauer ; illustrated by Brittany
   Baugus.
Description: Minneapolis, MN : Beaming Books, 2021. | Audience: Ages 5-8. |
   Summary: Relates how, since the first Christmas, animals around the
   world have been able to speak at midnight on Christmas Eve to rejoice
   and proclaim, "The Child is here!"
Identifiers: LCCN 2020056546 (print) | LCCN 2020056547 (ebook) | ISBN
   9781506466439 (hardcover) | ISBN 9781506466880 (ebook)
Subjects: CYAC: Human-animal communication--Fiction. | Jesus
   Christ--Nativity--Fiction. | Christmas--Fiction.
Classification: LCC PZ7.B3262 Ani 2021 (print) | LCC PZ7.B3262 (ebook) |
   DDC [E]--dc23
LC record available at https://lccn.loc.gov/2020056546
LC ebook record available at https://lccn.loc.gov/2020056547

VN0004589; 9781506466439; JUL2021

Beaming Books
PO Box 1209
Minneapolis, MN 55440-1209

Beamingbooks.com

A NOTE ABOUT THE LEGEND

The legend of animals talking on Christmas Eve probably grew out of another often-told tale. In that one, Jesus was said to have been born just as Christmas Eve turned into Christmas Day. Magical midnight occurrences gathered around that idea. The most lasting one was of animals being given the power of speech.

The animals' stories take different forms. The ox and the donkey are said to bow their heads at the stroke of midnight. Swarming bees hum a Christmas carol. One tale tells of the deer in the forest falling to their knees to honor the Great Spirit.

In one version, when the animals in the stable were given words, they quarreled. By the time they understood what they had witnessed, dawn had robbed them of speech and they could no longer praise.

Every one of these stories honors the birth of the Christ Child.

—M.D.B.